Look out! You're on thin ice!

"Moffitt! Watch out! The ice is cracking!" yelled Rusty Jackson.

Too late! *Crack*! The ice broke beneath Oliver's feet. The next thing he knew, Oliver was floundering around in icy water.

"Help!" he shouted. He was beginning to sink. He pumped his arms and legs to stay afloat.

"I'll go get help!" he heard Rusty shout.

But Oliver's water-soaked clothes were dragging him down. He could barely tread water now. His arms felt as if they were wrapped in lead.

"I'm drowning," he shouted, and his head went under.

Oliver's HIGH-FLYING ADVENTURE

MICHAEL McBRIER

Illustrated by Blanche Sims

Troll Associates

Library of Congress Cataloging in Publication Data

McBrier, Michael.
  Oliver's high-flying adventure.

  Summary: When Oliver reluctantly takes on a pet-
sitting job with a menagerie of birds during Christmas
vacation in which he had planned to compete in a snow-
sculpture contest, a naughty parrot escapes to further
complicate his life.
  [1. Birds—Fiction. 2. Pets—Fiction. 3. Snow
sculpture—Fiction] I. Sims, Blanche, ill. II. Title.
PZ7.M47830md   1987   [Fic]   86-16038
ISBN 0-8167-0820-7 (lib. bdg.)
ISBN 0-8167-0821-5 (pbk.)

OLIVER'S HIGH-FLYING ADVENTURE

CHAPTER
1

"**Y**oung man!" Oliver Moffitt turned around to find a stern-faced woman standing behind him. "What are you doing to that poor dog?"

"Nothing," said Oliver. "We're just taking a walk."

It was a cold windy day, and Oliver's dog, Pom-pom, had been hiding behind a tree. Now the little Shih Tzu began whimpering pitifully, his sad brown eyes staring up at the woman.

"The poor little thing must be freezing to death in that skimpy sweater."

Oliver had to admit, the red turtleneck sweater probably wasn't that warm. But Pom-pom hadn't minded it two minutes ago, when he'd been running around chasing papers.

"Pick up that dog this instant!" said the woman. "Some people don't know anything about taking care of pets!"

Oliver sighed and picked up Pom-pom. He *did* know about pets. In fact, he was the only kid in his school who had his own pet-care business. But he could see that this woman wouldn't listen.

Pom-pom scratched at Oliver's coat.

"He wants to get warm," said the woman. "Why don't you carry him inside your coat?"

Oliver knew better than to argue. "Yes, ma'am," he said, unzipping the coat. "I should take him home anyway."

Pom-pom squirmed in the coat until he was comfortable. Oliver scowled down at him. "What kind of animal are you anyway? You sleep so much, I think you're part bear. And the rest of the time you remind me of a little weasel."

Before he got a block away from the woman, Oliver heard someone calling his name. His friend and neighbor, Samantha Lawrence, was running toward him with a few of their classmates—Kimberly Williams, Matthew Farley, and Josh Burns.

"Hi," said Sam. She was wearing the new red cap Oliver had given her for Christmas. "What have you got there?" She pointed at his coat.

"Pom-pom," Oliver replied. "He decided he wanted a ride home."

"At least you have something to do," Kim said.

"Why aren't you with Jennifer?" Oliver asked. Usually, Kim Williams and Jennifer Hayes stuck together like glue.

"I don't do everything with Jennifer," said Kim. "Besides, we had a fight. I think we're getting bored with all this vacation time."

"Yeah," Sam said. "I thought it was great when they closed the school to fix the boiler.

But now there's nothing to do—except wish for snow."

Oliver nodded. "Yeah, then we could go sledding!"

"Haven't you heard about the snow-sculpture contest at Arrowhead Park?" Josh asked. "All the kids will be building statues out of snow on Great Pond. The best one wins a fifty-dollar prize. I'm going home to design something on my computer."

"Fifty dollars!" said Oliver. "Boy, could I use that."

"What about the money from your pet-care business?" asked Sam.

"I hit a slump just before Christmas. And I had so many bills to pay, they ate up all my money. I was going to get my mom an antique brass birdcage, but I didn't have enough money. So I had to borrow."

"Who did you borrow from?" asked Sam.

Oliver turned red. "From my mom," he mumbled.

Sam stared at him. "You borrowed from your own mother to get her Christmas present?"

"It's only temporary—until I start making money again," he explained. "But that prize money sure would help."

"Did you get a bird to keep in the cage?" Kim asked.

"That's what I wanted to do," Oliver said. "I thought I'd buy a canary or a parakeet. But Mom's going to put a plant in the birdcage instead."

"That'll look pretty," said Kim.

"I suppose so, after I get the cage all shiny. It looks pretty yucky now, but Mr. Huff gave me a good price because it was so messed up." Oliver felt Pom-pom stirring under his coat. "I should go home. Pom-pom is freezing, and I've got work to do!"

"I'd better head home too," said Matthew. "I've got to practice for my trumpet lesson."

"Yeah, it's getting late," said Kim. "I'll see you guys at Great Pond."

Oliver thought hard as he walked home with Sam. Then he stopped and turned toward her. "I have a super idea, but it'll take two of us to build it," he said. "We'll split the prize money— twenty-five dollars each. What do you think?"

"What's your super idea?" she asked.

"The Statue of Liberty. Life-size!" he said.

Sam gave him a look. "Do you know how big that is?"

"Okay, not life-size. But big! We'll have the biggest sculpture on the pond. It's sure to win."

"Okay, you've got a deal," said Sam. She did a cartwheel down the street toward her house. "Think snow!" she yelled.

Oliver was trying to find a weather forecast on the television, when his mother came home. She bent down and kissed him. He could smell the fresh air on her coat.

"Getting colder," Mrs. Moffitt said. "Brrr. A great night for hot soup."

Oliver opened the back door and looked up at the sky. Only a few stars glittered in the dark.

11

"Do you think it will snow?" he asked as his mother unloaded some groceries.

"Maybe," said Mrs. Moffitt. "But I hope not." She put butter and milk in the refrigerator, then smiled at him around the door. "Good news, Oliver. I've found a great pet-sitting job for you."

"What kind of pet?" asked Oliver. Mom's idea of something great would be a hamster.

"Something exotic and wonderful!"

Oliver raised his eyebrows. Maybe Mom really had found a rare animal. He'd already taken care of a camel and a monkey. "Exotic," he said, "like a gorilla or an elephant?"

"Exotic like *birds*. From South America, from Australia, from everywhere. A whole aviary full of birds."

"Aw, Mom," Oliver said disappointedly. "Birds are boring."

"I thought you'd jump at the chance," said Mrs. Moffitt. "You've been complaining for weeks about the slump in your business. Besides, I already promised that you'd do it."

A job was a job, Oliver thought. He just hoped it wouldn't take too much time away from the snow-sculpture contest.

"Who wants me to bird-sit?" Oliver asked.

"Frank Kirkby, my boss at the insurance agency," said Mrs. Moffitt. "He's heard so much about you, he's decided to let you take care of his birds. He and Mrs. Kirkby are going to Hawaii on vacation."

Mrs. Moffitt walked over to the sink. "Oliver! You promised you'd wash the dishes. I can't go to work *and* clean up after you."

Oliver ran back from the door. "Sorry, Mom. I meant to do them, but then—"

"Clean up that sink right now so I can start dinner. We're having cream of lettuce soup. It's a new recipe." Mrs. Moffitt looked around. "And where is Pom-pom?"

"Oh, he's—"

Before Oliver could finish, Pom-pom came skittering into the room, barking joyfully. Mrs. Moffitt scooped him up, and he covered her face with kisses.

Oliver turned on the faucet in the sink. How had all those dishes gotten in there? He'd had only breakfast, and lunch, and a couple of snacks. . . .

"Did you take Pom-pom for his walk?" Mrs. Moffitt asked.

Immediately, the dog ran to the door and started scratching.

"Yes, but he didn't—"

"Well, he wants to go now. Get his leash and sweater. You can do the dishes later."

Oliver ran to get his coat and Pom-pom's stuff.

"And what about that birdcage? Have you cleaned it up yet?"

"I meant to . . ." Oliver began, staring out at the rusty antique cage. It was on the floor beside the couch, holding open the encyclopedia to a section on the Statue of Liberty.

"Hurry up and take that poor dog out," Mrs. Moffitt insisted, tossing Pom-pom a dog biscuit. He caught it in midair with a snap of his jaws.

"You get away with everything," Oliver muttered, glaring at Pom-pom. "You lazy little weasel."

"Oliver!" said Mrs. Moffitt.

Oliver hurried out into the darkness. He knew he'd better get outside before his mother thought of something else he'd forgotten to do.

CHAPTER 2

The next afternoon Oliver climbed the steps of the Kirkby house and rang the bell.

"Mrs. Kirkby?" he said to the woman who opened the door. "I'm Oliver Moffitt. My mother told me you need a bird-sitter."

Mrs. Kirkby had short brown hair and a double chin. She wore white slacks and a floppy blue T-shirt that said, BE KIND TO YOUR FINE-FEATHERED FRIENDS. She smiled when she saw Oliver. "Wonderful!" she said. "Come and meet the kids."

They walked into a huge living room with a big stone fireplace. The aviary was in one corner of the room. It had a big glass panel in front and screens on the sides. Oliver saw something moving in the green leaves behind the glass. He glanced at Mrs. Kirkby. "I didn't know you had any kids—" he began.

"Bad boy!" screamed a voice.

Oliver spun around. Mrs. Kirkby smiled. "That's the biggest kid of all—Igor, my Amazon parrot." She walked over to a separate cage in the other corner of the room.

"Hello, Igor, you bad boy," she said. "This is Oliver. Do you want him to take care of you?"

"Wake up, stupid," Igor said. Mrs. Kirkby chuckled and glanced at Oliver.

Oliver stared at the bright-green bird in the cage. Its head was yellow except for a blue patch on its forehead.

"Why did he say that?" Oliver asked.

"Wake up, stupid!" Igor answered.

Mrs. Kirkby started laughing. "Whenever anyone asks him a question, he answers, 'Wake up, stupid!' " She shook her head. "It's a trick he learned from his last owner. At first I thought it was funny. But it does get a little tiresome." She sighed.

"He doesn't mean to be rude," Mrs. Kirkby continued. "Parrots don't really understand what they're saying."

"Uh, sure," Oliver said quickly. "I was just surprised, that's all."

Mrs. Kirkby led Oliver back to the aviary. They peered through the glass front to the plants inside. Just then, two birds came strutting across a green plastic rug that looked like grass.

"Casper and Jasper," said Mrs. Kirkby. "Button quail. They look so serious, don't they?"

Oliver smiled at the two birds. A flicker of movement toward the top of the aviary caught his eye. "Cheep!"

"That's Eddy. Or maybe Teddy," said Mrs. Kirkby. She pointed at a small gray and white bird with a red bill, sitting on a branch and looking at Oliver.

17

"Eddy and Teddy are zebra finches. I call them E and T for short."

"Cheep!"

Another zebra finch flew down and sat next to E. Or maybe T. They began to chatter as if they were talking to each other. Oliver laughed.

"They're a riot," he said.

Mrs. Kirkby slid open the front of the aviary and brought her finger up to the branch. "Come on, baby," she crooned. E climbed onto the finger. Mrs. Kirkby brought her hand over to Oliver. The bird on her finger cocked its head and stared.

"Cheep!" it said. Then it flew back to the aviary.

"That was a hello." Mrs. Kirkby smiled fondly as she closed the glass door. "They really are like my kids. My husband calls the aviary our 'flying circus.' "

Both E and T stared out at them.

"They may be shy with you at first, but they'll learn to trust you. Be gentle with them. Try not to make any quick movements, and always speak to them in a soft voice."

Oliver nodded, then watched carefully as Mrs. Kirkby showed him how the birds were fed and watered.

"What's that?" he asked, pointing to a small white shield on the side of the aviary. "It looks like some kind of seashell."

"Cuttlebone," replied Mrs. Kirkby. "It comes from the shell of the cuttlefish. Birds need it to get calcium. You'll have to replace it during the week we're away."

"Oh, yes," said Oliver. "Of course." He decided that he'd better read more about birds in his pet encyclopedia when he got home.

Mrs. Kirkby led Oliver out onto the back porch. "I keep the seed out here," she said. Oliver had his notebook ready, and he wrote down everything Mrs. Kirkby told him about what to feed the different birds. Finally, Mrs. Kirkby pointed to a plastic bucket filled with what looked like sand. "This is grit. It's very important for birds. They swallow it to grind up their food, since they have no teeth. So you must be sure to fill the grit cups every day."

"Every day," Oliver said as he wrote in his notebook. He sighed. That meant less time for the snow sculpture.

"It really is important," said Mrs. Kirkby. "An iddy-biddy bird can die in twenty-four hours if it isn't fed."

"No problem, Mrs. Kirkby," Oliver said. "Oliver Moffitt will get the job done!" But inside, he sighed.

Mrs. Kirkby opened the refrigerator. "The birds love greens. There are plenty in here. And you can give them an apple now and then—sliced, of course—and if you feel like it, some scrambled eggs once in a while. My kids just love treats. But don't leave eggs in the aviary too long." Oliver wrote quickly to keep up with her. He had no idea that birds were so fussy.

They walked back to the living room. First Mrs. Kirkby explained how to clean Igor's cage. Then she went over to the aviary, opened the door, and bent down.

"This little rug comes out. Take it outside and shake it out every couple of days. The wild birds will eat any leftover seeds. Then dip it into the tub upstairs and wash it."

Mrs. Kirkby had her back to Oliver, so she didn't see him nod his head. This aviary business was more work than he'd imagined. How was he going to find time to take care of the birds, build a snow sculpture—if it snowed—do his chores at home, take Pom-pom for walks— and have any fun? This was going to be some vacation!

"Oh, there's Miss Tootsie," said Mrs. Kirkby. "How are you, sweetie?"

A canary sat on a perch in the aviary and began to sing. E and T started chasing each other from branch to branch. Casper and Jasper were still strutting back and forth. And Oliver could see more movement among the leaves. "How many birds do you have?" he asked Mrs. Kirkby.

"Wake up, stupid!" Oliver jumped. Then he remembered Igor. He walked over to the cage.

Mrs. Kirkby closed the aviary and came over to him. "I used to have an even dozen, counting Igor," she said. "Then poor Millie died. We buried her under the forsythia in the garden. She was a lovebird." Mrs. Kirkby's eyes misted over. "We miss her. My birds are like children to me."

"Bad boy," said Igor, jumping to the side of his cage.

"You've got to be very careful with Igor," said Mrs. Kirkby. "His bill is strong and sharp.

He can give you a nasty bite. *Always* speak gently to him. And keep an eye on him when you clean his cage."

She grinned. "Parrots are real escape artists. Once he leaves this room, you may never find him! Luckily, he can't fly far, because his wings are clipped."

Mrs. Kirkby opened the cage and stuck her fist into it. Igor calmly stepped onto her wrist, and clung there while Mrs. Kirkby took her hand out of the cage.

"Bad boy," said Igor.

"Oliver's not a bad boy, Igor," Mrs. Kirkby said. "Won't you be nice to him while Mommy is away?"

"Wake up, stupid," Igor replied. Mrs. Kirkby sighed.

"Maybe I can teach him to say something else," Oliver said.

"If you can, I'll give you a special reward," said Mrs. Kirkby. "I've tried to teach him, but nothing seems to stick. I just wish Igor could say something *nice* once in a while. Can you imagine how angry he makes people by calling them 'stupid'?"

Igor flapped his wings. "Wake up, stupid!"

"I can guess," said Oliver as Igor went back into his cage.

Mrs. Kirkby smiled. "Now that we've finished talking business, how about some cookies and milk?"

Oliver nodded.

"Wait in the den. I'll be right back," she said, heading for the kitchen.

Oliver walked into the den and looked around the room. Framed photographs of birds sat on the piano. Paintings of birds hung on the walls. The only thing that didn't have birds on it was the television. That had a box with buttons and lights on top of it.

"Here we are." Mrs. Kirkby was carrying a tray. "Milk and my own homemade chocolate-chip cookies." She set it on the table.

"My favorite," said Oliver, taking a cookie. But his eyes were still on the box on top of the TV. "Is that a VCR?"

Mrs. Kirkby opened a cabinet beside the TV. It was filled with videotapes. "It certainly is. Every afternoon Igor and I watch a movie. His favorite is *Birdboy of Sing Sing*. But don't let him see *Canaries Are Forever*. It's much too violent."

She picked up a videotape. "This is how it works," she said.

"You mean I can use it?" Oliver said.

Mrs. Kirkby smiled. "Sure, but I have a selfish reason—I want you to spend as much time as possible here. The longer you stay, the better it is for my babies." She leaned forward. "Also, I'd like you to take in the mail every day and put it on the mantel. That way, no one will know we're out of town."

Oliver sat up straight. "No problem, Mrs. Kirkby. But would it be all right if I brought my mother's dog with me? I'm supposed to walk him every day."

Mrs. Kirkby reached for a cookie. "Certainly. But it's been so cold lately. Will your dog be

23

warm enough? I wouldn't want him catching cold and spreading germs to the kids."

"He has a turtleneck sweater," Oliver said.

Mrs. Kirkby thought for a moment. "You know, I have an old sheepskin jacket somewhere. Maybe your mother could make it into a coat for your dog. I'll leave the jacket in a shopping bag. You can take it home tomorrow."

"Gee, thanks, Mrs. Kirkby. I'll bet Pom-pom would like a nice warm coat."

"Good. Just remember to be careful with Igor. Never let him out of the cage when the dog is here. They might fight. I wouldn't want that. Igor's my special favorite. Aren't you, precious?"

"Wake up, stupid," squawked Igor.

Mrs. Kirkby stood up. "Well, I guess you're all ready then. Oh, I almost forgot." She pulled a piece of paper from her pocket. "This is where I get all my supplies. Just call this number if you ever have any questions about *anything*."

Oliver put the paper into his notebook and patted it. "No problem, Mrs. Kirkby. Your aviary is in good hands with Oliver Moffitt," he said. "At least it will be," he added to himself, "as soon as I read up on birds."

CHAPTER
3

Oliver biked over to the library the very next morning. He hurried along the shelves of the animal section. "Mammals, lizards . . . here we are. Birds." Oliver stopped at a book called *Your Precious Psittacine*. Parrots belonged to the psittacine family, he'd learned last night. But that was about all his pet encyclopedia had to say about birds.

Oliver pulled the parrot book down from the shelf. He also took *A Guide to Exotic Birds*. Then he found a book called *What Every Bird Owner Should Know*.

Oliver sat down at a table and leafed through the books. "Just what I need," he muttered. His eye caught a chapter titled, "Teach Your Parrot to Talk." Mrs. Kirkby had promised him something extra if he could teach Igor to say something new.

Quickly he read through the chapter. "No problem," he said to himself, closing the book. "It'll be a snap. What should I teach Igor to say?"

"Shhh!" said the librarian.

Oliver checked out the books and ran down the library steps. Then he dropped the books into his bicycle basket. It took him a while to undo the frozen lock on his bicycle, since it was a bitter cold day. Finally he heard it click.

But just as he was about to ride away, Oliver stopped. "Oh, no," he muttered. His old enemy, Rusty Jackson, was heading his way. Oliver wanted to pedal off fast, but Rusty wheeled his bike around and blocked his path.

"Hey, Moffitt," Rusty yelled. "Did you hear about the snow-sculpture contest? Bet I win."

Oliver sighed. Rusty was always making bets with Oliver, even though he always lost.

"No, you won't," said Oliver. "Sam and I are working on something stupendous. We're going to win hands down."

"Wanna bet?" Rusty asked.

"Yeah. I mean no," said Oliver. "I'm tired of betting with you, Rusty."

"You're just scared I'll win. Come on. Ten dollars against that new calculator of yours."

"Absolutely not," said Oliver. His mother had gotten him the calculator for Christmas. She'd kill him if he lost it. On the other hand . . . Oliver remembered the money he still owed his mother. Even if he and Sam won first prize in the snow-sculpture contest—and even after Mr. and Mrs. Kirkby paid him—he'd still need more money to get out of debt.

"Okay," said Oliver. "But wait till you see what Sam and I have planned."

"Some sissy thing, I'll bet," said Rusty.

"Don't call the Statue of Liberty a sissy thing," said Oliver. "Oops," he thought.

"The Statue of Liberty?" Rusty whooped with laughter. "You've gotta be kidding. You'll never be able to do that! It's impossible."

"Nothing is impossible!" Oliver replied.

"Well, I say it is!" Rusty looked down at the books in Oliver's basket.

"Hey, what are all those bird books for?"

"I'm reading up on birds. You might say my pet-care business is *branching out.*"

"Always thought you were *for the birds,* Moffitt." Rusty snickered.

"I've got a new job, working for the Kirkbys," Oliver said. "They've got an aviary full of exotic birds. And a parrot."

"Oh, yeah? I hear they've got a VCR too," Rusty said. "Is that true, Oliver old pal?"

"As a matter of fact, it *is* true," Oliver replied. "And I'm allowed to use it!"

"Really? Can I come over and watch with you?"

" 'Fraid not, Rusty. No strangers allowed in Mrs. Kirkby's house. And I don't know anybody *stranger* than you!"

"You hurt my feelings, Moffitt. But I'll bounce back. Maybe I'll even pop in and surprise you one day." Rusty smiled his sinister smile. "Statue of Liberty! You're a born loser!" He started his bicycle moving and rode off. "See ya!" he yelled.

Oliver sat very still, watching Rusty disappear. He wished he hadn't told Rusty about his new pet-sitting job. The last thing he needed

was for Rusty Jackson to show up at the Kirkby house.

Oliver shivered. It was getting colder, that was for sure. But the sky showed no signs of snow. And if it didn't snow soon, there'd be no snow-sculpture contest. That would mean no bet with Rusty. But it would also mean no twenty-five-dollar prize. And Oliver *really* needed that prize money.

"Let's go, snow," Oliver muttered as he pedaled home. "Let's go, snow!"

CHAPTER
4

Oliver rolled over in his bed and opened his eyes. It was strangely quiet. He looked at the clock.

"Omigosh," he said. "It's ten o'clock. It's really late. Mom's at work already."

He jumped out of bed and rolled up the window shade.

"Snow!" Oliver shouted.

Fat flakes were blowing against the dark sky. Oliver opened the window. A thin layer of snow lay on the sill. Oliver scooped some together, but it was too powdery to make into a snowball. He licked a snowflake on his arm. It tasted like metal. Oliver slammed the window shut and began to get dressed.

He had to get over to the Kirkby house right away. With all this snow and cold weather, the snow-sculpture contest could begin. And he wanted to get a good start with Sam. He looked over at the shiny calculator sitting on his desk. He'd sure hate to lose it to Rusty.

"Yap-yap." Pom-pom came bouncing into the room.

Oliver scratched Pom-pom's head. "Okay, Pom-pom, I know how you love to roll around in the snow. We'll go in a minute." Oliver glanced out the window. "Guess I'll have to take the bus to the Kirkbys' house today," he told the little dog. "That means you'll have to stay home."

Yesterday had been Oliver's first day on the job. He and Pom-pom had ridden over to the Kirkby house on his bicycle. Pom-pom paid no attention when Igor called him a bad boy. He'd just curled up near the radiator and slept until it was time to go home.

Today though, Oliver would have to take the bus. He sighed and wished he could go back to bed.

The snow was still falling later that afternoon when Oliver got off the bus at Great Pond. Even performing at top speed, bird-sitting chores had taken a long time. He ran over to the pond. He could see Sam's red cap in the distance.

"Hi, Oliver," called Jennifer Hayes, one of Oliver's classmates. "Isn't this fun?"

Jennifer was surrounded by bottles of purple liquid and patches of purple snow. Her mittens were stained purple too.

"What are you doing?" Oliver asked.

"I'm dying the snow purple for my sculpture." She sighed. "So far I've tried Magic Markers, grape juice, and food dyes. The problem is, when I wet the snow, it turns into ice."

"Why don't you make the sculpture first, then dye it?" Oliver suggested.

"Neat idea, Oliver. Thanks. I'll try that. Can you guess what I'm going to make?"

Oliver grinned. Everybody knew the Purple Worms was Jennifer's favorite rock group. "Nope," he said.

"A mess of purple worms! Isn't that a great idea? Kim said it was stupid. But she has no taste." Jennifer began scooping snow into a long, tubelike shape. "When I win the prize, I'm going to take a picture and send it to the real Purple Worms. They'll love it. Don't you think?"

Josh Burns dashed up to Oliver and Jennifer. "Hey, Oliver. Want to help me with my robot? I'm covering the whole thing with aluminum foil."

"Sorry, Josh. Sam and I are supposed to be working together on a sculpture. Maybe later if I have time."

"Sure. I can't wait till I get to the head. I'm going to use light bulbs for eyes."

"Sounds terrific," Oliver said. "What's that?" He pointed to a big square of cardboard set up on the pond. "It looks like a wall."

"It is. Rusty Jackson put a fence around his sculpture. Doesn't want anyone to know what he's doing. That's why he's working all the way out there in the middle of the pond."

Oliver shook his head. "Just like Rusty," he said. "I'd better get over to Sam." Oliver waved and walked away. He looked over his shoulder and stared at Rusty's fence. "What could he be building?" Oliver wondered. "A dinosaur? Or maybe he's doing the Empire State Building. That's even bigger than the Statue of Liberty! Leave it to Rusty to steal our idea—sort of."

Oliver was so lost in thought that he almost bumped into Kim Williams. She was pushing a shopping cart full of things.

"Hey, Kim. What's all that stuff?" Oliver asked.

"Cleaned out my closet. Under the bed too," said Kim.

"But what are you going to use all this stuff for?"

Kim sighed. "Props for my sculpture. But I've got too many ideas. So I figured I'd experiment with everything until I saw something that really works."

Oliver thought for a moment. "Did you think about making a boa constrictor?" Kim's older brother Parnell owned a boa named Squeeze Me.

Kim shook her head. "Too much like Jennifer's worms. That's why we had a fight. She said I don't know anything about music because I said I didn't like the Purple Worms' latest record."

She reached into the cart and pulled out a hockey stick. "Maybe I'll do a hockey player," she muttered. She bent over the cart and rummaged deeper.

Oliver shrugged. Sam was waving at him. He trotted over to where she had already piled up a heap of snow.

"Oliver, look. This is going to be Miss Liberty's pedestal. But we need more snow."

Oliver bent down and began shoving snow

toward Sam's pile. It soon began to get bigger and bigger.

"I think that's enough for the base," Sam said. She took off her cap and wiped her face with her scarf. "This is *hard* work." She bent her head back and let the snow fall on her face.

"Time for a break," said Josh. He'd strolled over with Matthew Farley, another classmate.

"This is fun," said Matthew. "I'm making a snowman with a black belt." He went into a karate position and grunted.

Oliver grinned. Matthew was taking karate lessons.

"How's the bird-sitting, Oliver?" Sam asked.

"It's okay. This was my second day on the job."

"Sam told me you were going to try to teach the Kirkbys' parrot to talk," Josh said.

"He can say some things already," Oliver said. "But I want to teach him something *polite* to say."

"Let me know if I can help. I'm reading up on artificial speech and computers," Josh said. "Did you know that computers can talk, but they can't understand people when people talk to them?"

"It's sort of like that with Igor," Oliver said, laughing. "*Your Precious Psittacine* said I had to repeat the word over and over that I want Igor to learn. I must have said my name a hundred times. And all that dumb parrot says back is 'Ah.' It's hard work."

"Have you used the Kirkbys' VCR yet?" asked Sam.

"Sure. I watched two movies with Igor yesterday: *Paloma the Parrot Girl* and *Wings over Westport*. Mrs. Kirkby has lots of bird movies."

"Do you really have to go over there every day?" Matthew asked.

Oliver nodded. He shoved snow over to the base with his foot.

"And guess who I saw yesterday? The Cat Lady! She was setting out little dishes of food for the stray cats near the Kirkby house." Oliver laughed. The Cat Lady took care of all the stray cats in town. "She told me it's hard for cats to find food in the winter. No birds."

Sam grinned. "If only they knew what was inside the Kirkby house."

"Hey, Oliver! Do the Kirkbys have a tape of *Attack of the Killer Chickens*?" Josh asked. "Or *Computer Madness*? I'd love to see them again."

"They probably do. Mrs. Kirkby told me her husband is a real science fiction fan. He has all those movies."

"Could we come over and watch them?" Josh asked.

"I'd love to see *Killer Chickens* again," Sam said.

"And I'd like to see *The Kung Fu Kid*," Matthew said.

"It'd be great if all of you could come with me. I can't ride a bike in all this snow and I hate taking that long bus ride all alone. Besides, filling all those cups and bottles takes forever. We could get done in a flash if we worked together. But—"

"Great," Sam interrupted. "Let's meet at the

bus stop at ten o'clock tomorrow morning. Then we can come back here."

Suddenly Oliver felt a blow to his back. He spun around.

"How's my new calculator, Moffitt?" said Rusty, brushing what was left of a snowball from the back of Oliver's jacket.

"It's not yours yet, Rusty," said Oliver. "And it never will be."

"Bet you haven't made much progress on your Statue of Liberty, have you?"

"I've got to run," Matthew said. "See you tomorrow." He dashed off.

"What are you doing behind that fence, Rusty? Why all the secrecy?" Josh asked.

"Great designers always keep their plans a secret," Rusty answered. "You'll see on the day of the contest."

Rusty turned to Sam. "You guys are going to be sorry. You've got a big problem with that Statue of Liberty. And you don't even know it yet."

"What do you mean?" asked Sam.

"You'll see," said Rusty. "Wait till you get to the arm with the torch." Rusty laughed and headed for the middle of the pond.

Everyone was quiet. "Uh-oh," said Josh. "I think Rusty has a point. How can you make a snow arm strong enough to hold up the torch? It's too heavy. It will all fall off."

Oliver stared in horror. "Whoever heard of a Statue of Liberty with no torch?"

"Or no arm?" said Sam. She shook her head.

"But I have a plan—and if it works, Miss Liberty will hold her torch up high!"

Oliver thought about his calculator and hoped that Sam's idea would work. If he lost it, he'd never be able to go back home—and it was awfully cold out.

CHAPTER
5

The next day Oliver and his friends got to work at the Kirkby house.

"Hey, Sam. Want to help me with Igor's cage?" asked Oliver.

"Wake up, stupid," said Igor.

"Oh, hush, Igor," said Sam. She steadied the cage while Oliver removed the bottom. Then he lifted the cage from its hook and set it on some newspaper on the floor. Igor sat on a perch, still inside.

"I'll go upstairs to rinse this off and put down fresh paper," said Oliver, heading for the stairway.

"And I'll pick up the rug in the aviary," said Sam. "Too bad Matthew couldn't make it. He'd enjoy this."

Sam slid the glass panel open. Casper and Jasper were pacing back and forth. Sam stood for a moment, wondering how she could remove the carpet while the birds were on it. She gently tugged it toward her. With great dignity

Casper and Jasper stepped off the rug. Sam folded it in half and closed the glass panel.

"Open the door, please, Josh," she called. "I have to take this outside."

Josh had just walked into the living room, balancing a lettuce leaf full of scrambled eggs. The doorbell rang.

"Who can that be?" asked Sam. Josh opened the front door.

"Hi, it's us," screamed Jennifer and Kim. They pushed past Josh, knocking his scrambled eggs onto the porch. "Rusty invited us over to see movies on the VCR."

"Oh, no," said Oliver. He ran down the stairs as Rusty walked in.

"Hi, old pal!" said Rusty, walking in. "Where's the VCR?"

"Wake up, stupid," said Igor.

Rusty wheeled around. "Who said that?"

"Bad boy," said Igor.

Sam laughed and pointed at Igor. "You sure got *that* one right, Igor." She was still laughing as she put the carpet back into the aviary.

Rusty walked over to Igor's cage and looked down.

Igor stared up at Rusty. "Bad boy," he said again. "Stupid."

"Why, you dumb excuse for a . . . for a . . ." Rusty shouted. He yanked the cage up from the floor. Igor stalked out from under it and pecked Rusty's shoe.

"Get away!" yelled Rusty, jumping back.

His heel caught on the carpet, and he fell backward. The cage swung high in the air.

Smash! It hit the glass panel on the aviary. Oliver watched, helpless, as the glass shattered.

"Oh, no," moaned Sam. Casper and Jasper gingerly stepped over the broken glass and strutted out of the aviary and under a chair. E and T flew out. Soon the room was full of birds.

"Watch out! They're attacking!" cried Kim as E and T chased her into the kitchen. She slammed the door behind her. E and T wheeled around in the air while Igor stalked Rusty, step by step.

"Get that parrot away from me," yelled Rusty, walking backward. "Yeow!" he cried as he fell over a shopping bag near the door.

Brightly colored birds were fluttering all around the room. E and T did loop the loops with each other, chattering happily.

"Yow!" said Sam. "How will we ever catch them?"

As Rusty stood up, Miss Tootsie, the canary, swooped toward him. Rusty covered his head with his arms. "Where's that dumb parrot?" he asked. His back was against the wall, near the front door.

Oliver looked around wildly. Where *was* Igor?

Rusty jumped over the shopping bag and dashed for the door. He ran out, not even stopping to close the door behind him.

Oliver rushed after him, then skidded to a stop beside the overturned shopping bag. "Pompom's new winter coat," he muttered, seeing the sheepskin sticking out of the bag. He bundled the coat back in. "Josh, shut that door."

Josh grabbed the knob, then hesitated. The

Cat Lady was standing on the sidewalk. She was watching a cat eat the scrambled eggs Josh had dropped earlier.

"How kind of you," she said. "But cats don't eat lettuce, you know."

"Um, I'll remember that," Josh said. He took one more glance at the cat, then quickly shut the door. "I'll bet he's hungry," Josh muttered. "That's the last thing we need in here—a hungry cat!"

Jennifer began to sneeze. "I forgot. I'm ah–ah–ah–CHOO! Allergic. To feathers."

She ran to the front door. "Oh, hello," she said when she saw the Cat Lady. Jennifer sneezed again. The cat looked up and ran between Jennifer's legs. Jennifer slammed the door behind her, but it was too late. The cat was in the house.

"How many birds are loose?" Josh asked.

"Ten. Plus Igor," Oliver said. He shook his head. "Igor! Where are you?" he called. "And what is that cat doing in here?" He froze. "A cat!" he yelled. "Get him away from the birds!"

Sam and Josh tried to shoo the birds to the other side of the room, but wherever the birds went, the cat followed.

Oliver stared up at the ceiling. E and T were still doing aerial acrobatics between the wooden beams. Casper and Jasper were calmly sitting under the chair. But for how long? Oliver raced the cat to the chair and picked up a bird in each hand.

"Now what?" he asked, dodging Sam as she chased the cat under a table.

Josh saw a wicker wastebasket. "Put the birds under here for a while," he said, flipping it upside down.

Oliver nodded and placed Casper and Jasper under the overturned basket. "Let's catch some more!" he said.

While Oliver tried to coax another bird down from the chandelier, Sam cornered the cat under the table.

"Ah-ha!" she crowed. She lifted the wastebasket and popped it over the cat. "Got you now!"

Casper and Jasper waddled off.

Oliver walked up to the basket with another bird in his hand.

"Stop!" cried Sam as he was about to put the bird inside. "I've got the cat in there!"

"But I had birds in—" Oliver stopped. Cat yowls were coming from inside the wastebasket. Then it toppled over and the cat streaked out. The bird in Oliver's hand flew away.

"This isn't getting us anywhere," Oliver muttered.

"I have an idea," said Sam. "I'll go back to your house and get that old birdcage. You can put the birds in there until the aviary is fixed."

"Good idea," he said. "Look here." Against the wall was a red wooden chest. Oliver lifted the lid. "It's empty. We can put some birds in here temporarily. You go get the cage."

Kim peered out of the kitchen. "Are they gone yet?"

"And—uh—you can take Kim along to help," Oliver said. "Josh and I will catch the birds."

Josh had rounded up Casper and Jasper again and put them into the box. He propped the top open a crack with *A Guide to Exotic Birds*. "They'll need air," he said.

"They'll probably fall asleep in the dark," Oliver said.

He spotted the cat, sitting on the floor in front of the sofa. It was eyeing E and T, who had finally tired of flying and were perched on a curtain rod.

As Oliver rushed to the sofa, he noticed Sam putting on her coat.

"Wait," said Oliver. "I was supposed to take that sheepskin jacket to my mother. Can you take it with you?"

"Sure," said Sam. She picked up the shopping bag and dashed out of the house. Kim ran after her, holding her hands over her head.

Josh had climbed up on the sofa and was reaching for E on the curtain rod. E flew away, so Josh put his finger in front of T. T grasped Josh's finger.

"Tickles," Josh said. He stepped down from the sofa and put T into the red chest. Balancing Oliver's book on the edge, he slowly lowered the lid.

"It works," he said. "Open enough for air, but not enough to escape."

"Where's the cat?" Oliver asked.

"Staring into the fireplace," said Josh.

Oliver dashed over. Miss Tootsie was sitting on the fire screen. Oliver reached out and gently picked her up.

"She's frightened. I can feel her heart beat-

45

ing." He put Miss Tootsie into the red chest with T.

"The cat can actually help us," said Josh. "All we have to do is look where *he's* looking, and we'll find a bird. We should call him Sherlock."

In a little over an hour, Oliver and Josh had rounded up nine of the birds. E was still missing.

"No problem," said Oliver. "Sherlock will find him."

Josh got a broom. He began to sweep the broken glass onto the newspaper that had been under Igor's cage. The cage was still on the floor.

"Where's Igor?" Josh asked.

"Igor! I forgot all about him! Where is he?" Oliver looked around the room. Near the front door lay two bright-green feathers. Oliver looked at the cat. He was licking his paws.

"Oh, no! You don't suppose—?" Oliver began.

"Naw. Igor's too tough. He'd eat the cat before the cat ate him!"

Oliver wanted to believe Josh. But he wasn't sure. "Where is he, then?"

"Maybe he flew out when the door was open," Josh said.

"Then he'll die. Parrots can't survive in the cold," Oliver said. He sank down on the sofa and stared at Igor's empty cage. Maybe if he just left the cage on the floor Igor would go back into it. That's if Igor was in the house—and still alive. And if he wasn't? What would he tell Mrs. Kirkby?

The doorbell rang. It was Sam with the birdcage.

Within minutes they'd taken the birds out of the chest and put some of them into the antique cage. The others went into Igor's cage.

"Kind of crowded," said Oliver. "But safe enough for a while."

"Cheep."

"What's that?" asked Sam.

"Sounds like E," said Josh. The three of them began to search the room. The cat was asleep near the fireplace.

"No luck," said Sam, peering into the chandelier.

"Cheeep."

Josh was looking behind a picture. "It must be over there," he said, pointing to the fireplace.

"Cheeeep." Sherlock opened an eye.

Oliver looked in the fireplace. Then he got a chair and looked behind the mail on the mantel. He reached for a vase and peered in. "Look!" he cried. Deep inside the vase lay E.

"Cheep."

Oliver reached into the vase and eased the bird out. "Time to join your brother." He jumped down from the chair and put the finch into the cage.

"What are you going to do about replacing the glass?" Sam asked.

Oliver groaned and sank down on the sofa again. "I guess I'll have to call someone to fix it," he said.

"I'll get the phone book," Josh said. "I saw one in the kitchen." He left the room.

"What am I going to do about Igor?" Oliver asked. "Mrs. Kirkby will be heartbroken. Igor was her special favorite. If he's lost, I'll have to buy the Kirkbys a new parrot. It'll probably cost hundreds of dollars. I'll be wiped out."

"I'm sorry, Oliver," Sam said. "I wish I could help." She walked over to the sleeping cat. "At least we can get rid of him."

Sam opened the door and set the cat down on the porch. He ran down the steps. "Sherlock's headed for the house next door," Sam said, looking out the door.

"He probably lives there," Oliver said. "Hey, Sam, I don't suppose you happen to see a green parrot with a yellow head and a blue patch out there, do you?"

"No parrots at all. But I see the Cat Lady across the street." Sam ran outside. She was back a few minutes later.

"I asked the Cat Lady if she'd seen Igor. But all she saw was a lot of kids running in and out of the house. No bird."

"Well, where can he be?" Oliver asked.

Josh came into the living room holding the telephone directory. He sat down next to Oliver and pointed to an ad. "Yukon Glass," he said. "My mother used them last summer to fix a broken window. She said they did a pretty good job."

Oliver took the book and stared at the list of glass specialists. He didn't feel like doing anything.

"I hate to leave you in the lurch," Sam said.

"But it's getting late. We've still got a lot of work to do on our snow sculpture."

"Right," Oliver said. "You and Josh go to Great Pond. I'll call Yukon Glass and wait here for the glazier to show up. If there's time, I'll see you at the pond." Oliver stood up. "And while I'm waiting, I'll search the house for Igor. He's got to be in here somewhere!"

"I wish I could stay and help," Sam said. "But the contest is the day after tomorrow."

"I'm sorry, Sam," Oliver said. "I'll try to be at Great Pond as soon as I can."

Sam shrugged. She opened the front door. "Good luck, Oliver," she said.

"Call me tonight if you need help," Josh said. "Maybe I could print posters about Igor on my computer. We could hang them up in the neighborhood."

"No! Don't do that! Not yet! I don't want anyone to know we've lost him. Mrs. Kirkby told me Igor was an escape artist. I'll find him if it takes me all afternoon."

"See you later," Sam and Josh said together. They ran down the porch steps. Oliver watched until they were out of sight around the corner. He wished he could go with them.

But he had work to do.

Back in the house, Oliver took the phone book and went into the kitchen. He dialed the number for Yukon Glass. It rang six times.

"Yukon Glass," said a voice at last. "Glass for every need. Fred speaking. May I help you?"

Oliver cleared his throat and made his voice

50

as deep as possible. He didn't want Fred to know he was just a kid. He explained the problem.

"Thank you for calling, Mr. Moffitt," Fred said. "We'll be there at noon tomorrow."

"Tomorrow?" Oliver's voice squeaked. He brought it under control. "You mean you can't come today?"

"All our trucks are out. Seems a lot of windows are getting broken these days. All those kids on vacation. I guess they have nothing better to do than throw snowballs." Fred chuckled. "But it *is* good for business."

"I'm sure it is," Oliver said. "By the way, how much will the glass cost?"

"Depends on the size of the glass and the labor required to cut it to fit," said Fred. "Probably in the forty-dollar ballpark."

"Forty," Oliver croaked.

"Or more," Fred said. "See you at noon. Have a nice day." He hung up.

Oliver groaned. Where was he going to get all that money?

CHAPTER
6

It was dark by the time Oliver caught the bus home. He'd searched the Kirkby house from top to bottom, but had not found Igor. Now he had to get home before his mother did and take Pom-pom for his walk.

As the bus passed Great Pond, Oliver wondered how Sam was doing with the statue. How could he get half the prize unless he did half the work? Now he needed the prize money more than ever.

As soon as Oliver walked into his house, Pom-pom came running up to him.

Pom-pom ran in circles around Oliver, barking. He seemed more excited than usual.

Oliver quickly fetched Pom-pom's leash and turtleneck sweater. He tried to put them on, but Pom-pom ran away from him toward the cellar door. The door was slightly open. Oliver slammed it shut.

"You've got to go outside," Oliver said. But Pom-pom planted his feet at the cellar door and kept barking. Oliver got a dog biscuit. Using it as a lure, he finally managed to get the sweater and leash on Pom-pom and take him outside.

By the time Pom-pom was ready to go back in, he was shivering. Oliver picked him up and held him close. "No wonder you didn't want to go out," he said. "Your turtleneck really *isn't* warm enough, is it?" Pom-pom licked Oliver's face.

They went inside the house. "Don't worry, Pom-pom! You'll soon have a new sheepskin coat. I wonder where Sam put the shopping bag." Oliver let Pom-pom run loose while he looked around the living room. Then he went into the kitchen.

Oliver had just begun washing the dishes, when his mother came home.

"Did you take Pom-pom for his walk?" she asked.

"Wake up, stupid," said a familiar voice.

Oliver froze.

"What did you say?" Mrs. Moffitt asked angrily.

"Bad boy," Oliver heard.

"You certainly are. How dare you call me stupid!" His mother was tapping her foot.

"I didn't," Oliver stammered. "I mean, I was talking to myself. I'm so tired. I was just telling myself to wake up." He gave his mother a weak grin.

She looked concerned. "You *are* working hard," she said. "How's it going at the Kirkbys?"

Oliver decided not to tell his mother what had happened. Especially since Mr. Kirkby was her boss. She might lose her job because of him. He hadn't thought of that. He groaned softly.

"Are you all right?" his mother asked. She put her hand on his forehead. "You're flushed," she said. "You may have a fever. Go upstairs, take a hot bath, and get into bed. You need rest."

"Bad boy," Oliver heard again.

"No, you're not. Stop saying that. You're the best son a mother ever had." Mrs. Moffitt hugged Oliver.

He wanted to cling to her, and tell her all his troubles. But he couldn't. She had enough on her mind. He looked up at her and smiled.

"Go to bed," his mother said. "I'll bring up some nice hot soup for you later. Now, scoot." She slapped him playfully on the seat.

Oliver went upstairs and ran some hot water for his bath. "Igor must be in the house," Oliver thought. He tiptoed down the hall and eased open the door to his mother's room. Pom-pom was snoring in the middle of the bed.

"Some watchdog," Oliver muttered. "Igor could be perched on his nose, and he'd never know it." Still on tiptoes, Oliver searched the room. Pom-pom never moved.

Oliver spent several more minutes checking out the whole top floor. Then he remembered he'd left the water running in the tub. He hurried back to the bathroom and turned off the water. It was about to overflow, so he drained some out and then got in.

As he soaped himself, Oliver tried to think. Igor wasn't upstairs. He hadn't been in the kitchen, and Oliver hadn't seen him in the living room. But he might be under the sofa or even behind the refrigerator. There were lots of places an escape artist could hide, especially if he was as small as Igor. So where was he?

Oliver finished his bath, got out of the tub, and began drying himself. He listened to the water gurgling out of the tub. Then he had a chilling thought. What if Igor were dead?

"Just my luck," Oliver said to himself. "I'm probably being haunted by a parrot ghost." He imagined Igor, draped in a sheet, stalking him down the hallway. That gave him an idea. He opened the door to the linen closet.

"Ah-ah-ah!" he heard.

That was no ghost! It was Igor! But where? Not in the linen closet, the sound was too far away.

"Ah-ah-ah!" the voice went on.

"Gargling, Oliver?" his mother asked from downstairs. "That's a good idea. You don't want to get a sore throat."

"Right, Mom," Oliver yelled. He went to his room and pulled on his pajamas. They were bright-red flannel. His grandmother had sent them for Christmas. They made Oliver feel warm and toasty—they made him feel drowsy too.

Oliver pulled down the bed covers. He'd have to wait until his mother fell asleep. Then he could search the whole house. Oliver yawned.

"Now, how do I make myself stay awake?" He crawled into bed. "Nothing is going right." He began to add up how much money he owed. Then he subtracted how little he would earn. If he didn't get Igor back to the Kirkbys, he'd be in debt for life.

It felt so good to be lying down. Oliver closed his eyes. "Just for a moment," he said.

"Wake up, stupid," he heard as from a great distance.

"Bad boy. Bad boy," Oliver muttered.

"My poor sweetheart," he heard his mother say. "You're having a nightmare. And talking in your sleep. You must be sick." She helped Oliver sit up, and plumped his pillows.

Oliver looked at her groggily. He had fallen asleep.

His mother set a tray down on his lap. "Thanks, Mom," he said. "Mmmm, delicious. Onion soup is my favorite!"

Mrs. Moffitt smiled. "Sam called you earlier. She said to call her back if you felt up to it."

Poor Sam! Oliver knew he wouldn't get to the pond until late tomorrow. If Yukon Glass came at noon, Oliver would be lucky to make it by two. "Maybe it's my idea, but it's not fair to make her do all the work," Oliver thought.

"Lost your appetite, dear?" his mother asked. "That's the fever. Try to eat as much as you can. Then go back to sleep."

Oliver ate a mouthful of soup. "Wake up, stupid," he heard. He grinned. His mother grinned back. She kissed him on the forehead and left the room.

"Got to keep up my strength," Oliver muttered. He peeled a piece of melted cheese off the side of the bowl and ate it. He dipped the spoon into the soup. It wasn't long before the

bowl was empty. Balancing the tray, he got out of bed. He set the tray on his desk.

As he dialed Sam's number, he remembered he still hadn't paid the telephone bill for this month. It was expensive, running your own business.

Sam finally answered the phone. Oliver filled her in on what Fred the glazier had said.

Sam groaned. "What about the sculpture? Josh and Kim helped me pile up snow for the body. I think we've got enough to start carving the drapes on her dress."

"By the way, I looked up how tall the *real* Statue of Liberty is," Oliver said. "Including the pedestal, it's over three hundred feet high!"

"We'd need all the snow in town for that!" Sam gasped. "Ours is only six feet tall, including the base."

"Sounds big enough to win," Oliver said. "By the way, Sam, what are we doing about the arm and torch?"

"I talked my idea over with Josh. He called it an armature."

"What's that?" asked Oliver.

"An inside support. I'm going to use Kim's hockey stick. She's not using it now, since she's working with Jennifer. I figure if I pack the snow all around it, the stick will hold the arm up."

"Great!" said Oliver. "We've got to win this contest. I really need the money now."

"How much will the new glass cost?" Sam asked.

"Fred said the new glass would cost about

forty dollars. Cash on delivery." Oliver groaned. "I told him to go ahead, and I don't even have the money."

"*I've* got forty dollars," Sam said. "My uncle Walter sent it to me for Christmas. I'm not supposed to spend it, but I'll lend it to you."

"Oh, Sam. You're a lifesaver. If you could lend it to me, you know I'll pay you back."

"With your half of the prize money, right?"

"And my bird-sitting fee—or part of it," Oliver said.

"I'll drop the money in your mailbox tonight," Sam told Oliver.

"Good. I'll go to the Kirkbys first thing tomorrow," Oliver said. "Maybe Fred will come before noon. As soon as he leaves, I'll head for Great Pond."

"Okay, Oliver," said Sam. "We'll have everything fixed tomorrow. So long." She hung up.

Oliver put his phone down. "Everything fixed," he sighed, looking at the calculator on his desk. "Not quite, Sam!"

CHAPTER
7

The next morning Oliver found a note on the kitchen table.

Hope you're feeling better. Don't go out unless you feel well. Call me if you need anything.

Love,
Mom

P.S. You were tossing and turning and talking in your sleep all night. You're not stupid. And you're _not_ a bad boy. Hugs and kisses.

Oliver glanced at the clock. It was after nine. He had to rush. He ate a quick breakfast and then got dressed.

"Pom-pom," he called. Where was that dog? Never could find him when you wanted him.

"Yap-yap." Pom-pom ran up from the cellar.

"What were you doing down there? Come on, we've got to hurry."

Oliver put on Pom-pom's leash and sweater and took him for a short walk. As usual, Pom-pom didn't want to stay out for long. Back in the house, the little dog curled up near the radiator.

Oliver noticed that the shopping bag with the sheepskin jacket was in the corner of the living room. "That must be how Igor got here," Oliver said out loud. "Sam carried him over. But where is he now?"

Another look at the clock. It was after ten. Oliver pulled on his mittens and left the house. He walked to the mailbox and took out the envelope Sam had left for him. Two twenty-dollar bills. Good old Sam. Oliver dashed to the corner for the bus.

By the time he got to the Kirkby house, it was nearly eleven. As soon as he took off his coat, he went over to the aviary. He'd put the birdcages in there yesterday so the birds would feel at home.

E and T were swinging on a perch in the antique cage. "Cheep," said E. "Cheep," said T. Or maybe it was the other way around.

"Hi, gang," he said. He gave the cages a quick inspection. All the birds were alive and looked healthy. He checked the seed cups and water bottles. He had a lot to do.

Before he knew it, it was twelve. Oliver went

to the window and looked out. No sign of Fred. Oliver shrugged. Nobody was ever on time.

An hour later Oliver made himself lunch— scrambled eggs and an apple. By three o'clock the glazier still hadn't arrived. Oliver found some paper and a pencil in the kitchen and began to doodle.

At ten minutes to four a truck pulled into the driveway.

"Mr. Moffitt?" the glazier asked when Oliver opened the door.

"My—er—father had to go out," Oliver said. "There's the aviary." Fred went over to it and took out a folding ruler. He measured the door and then went out to his truck. A short while later he brought in a big piece of glass, which he'd cut to size in the truck. He fit it into the aviary and stood back.

Oliver let the birds out of the cages. They flew happily around their home. Casper and Jasper began strutting on the carpet again.

"Looks great," Fred said. "Sorry I was late. Had an emergency call. People were freezing. That'll be forty-three dollars and fifty cents." He held out his hand.

"But that's all the money I have on me," Oliver croaked. "I need some change for the bus."

"Okay. Forty-three. Where are you headed?"

"Great Pond," said Oliver. "I'm building a snow sculpture for the contest."

"That's on my way," Fred said. "I'll give you a ride."

As he sat in the glazier's truck, Oliver began to worry. It was so late. Sam had probably gone home by now. And he had to be home by five to walk Pom-pom. When was he going to find the time to search for Igor? Oliver moaned.

"You okay, kid?" Fred asked. "We're almost there."

"I'm fine," Oliver said. "Just fine."

He stared thoughtfully out the window until the truck stopped. Oliver thanked the driver and headed for the pond, his feet crunching on the snow.

Rusty's cardboard fence was still up in the middle of the pond. "What *was* he up to?" Oliver wondered. Jennifer's purple worms writhed and coiled in a heap. They looked eerily real in the fading light.

Next came Josh's robot, which now stood four feet high. It was square and had an antenna made out of a pair of ice tongs. It was almost finished except for the aluminum-foil wrapping and the light-bulb eyes, but it was wearing Josh's blue scarf around its neck.

Matthew's karate-man statue was next to the robot. Mr. Karate looked like a regular snow-man—except he was wearing a black belt around the waist. Oliver smiled. They were all super sculptures.

Then he saw Miss Liberty. She was almost done! Sam had even put an aluminum-foil crown on top of her head. "How did she get it up there?" Oliver wondered. She held a book in her left arm. The only thing missing was her right arm with the torch. Kim's hockey stick lay near the statue.

"Poor Sam," Oliver whispered. "Looks like she tried but couldn't get that armature thing to work."

He packed some snow around the hockey stick, but it kept falling off. Then he remembered the trouble Jennifer was having. Maybe if he and Sam wet the stick first and then packed the snow, it would hold. He'd bring a bottle of water tomorrow, and they'd try it. He leaned the hockey stick against the statue and stepped back.

Miss Liberty looked wonderful. It was the tallest sculpture on the pond. They were sure to win. If only they could get the arm in place. He'd call Sam later and tell her his idea. Oliver looked around. He was all alone.

He walked out to the middle of the pond, where Rusty's secret sculpture was hiding behind its wall. Any second he expected Rusty to jump out at him. But nothing happened. Oliver circled the cardboard fence several times. When he could no longer stand the suspense, he took a peek behind it.

There, sitting on the ice, was an almost life-size replica of an old car. Rusty had used pie plates for headlights and an old bicycle tire for a steering wheel. It had a real aerial sticking up in front and big old-fashioned tail fins in the back. Oliver's heart sank. Rusty's car was a winner. A real winner!

Oliver began to trudge home. At long last,

Rusty would win a bet—*and* Oliver's calculator. Then his heart *really* sank as he remembered his *biggest* problem. Igor was still missing!

CHAPTER
8

"**W**ake up, stupid!"

Oliver sat up in bed. That Igor! Where was he? Last night Oliver had sat and watched TV while his mother worked on Pom-pom's new sheepskin coat. Every now and then he'd gone off and searched a different room in the house. But no luck. To make matters worse, his mother had even scolded him for saying "Wake up, stupid" so often.

Oliver hopped out of bed. He heard dripping. Outside. He looked out the window.

"Oh, no," he groaned. Drops of water clung like jewels to the branches of trees. He could see muddy patches on the lawn, where snow had melted.

The business phone rang. It was Sam.

"Oliver! Did you see what happened? A thaw!"

"What about the contest?" Oliver asked. "Do you think it's still on? Today's the big day."

"I don't know. Let's get over there quick to see if anything is left of our statue!"

Oliver threw on some clothes. He grabbed

Pom-pom and put the old turtleneck on him. "Too warm for your new coat, old fella," he said. With Pom-pom under his arm, he ran to the garage for his bicycle. He plopped Pom-pom into the basket and wheeled the bicycle down the driveway. Sam was waiting for him. She had on a jacket but no cap. "At least we can use our bicycles," she said. "The snow's all melted."

They hopped on their bicycles and pushed off. In minutes they were at Great Pond. No one else was there yet.

"What a mess," said Sam. They had trouble making their bicycles stand in the slush at the edge of the pond.

Oliver held Pom-pom tight. "Look," he said. "Jennifer's purple worms. They look like grape juice."

"Come on," said Sam. She began running toward Miss Liberty. Oliver looked down at the ice and stamped his foot. The ice seemed pretty thick, but a thin layer of slush covered the top. He set Pom-pom down.

"Yap-yap," barked Pom-pom. He turned and headed for the shore.

"Sorry," Oliver yelled. "Forgot you hate to get your feet wet."

Oliver caught up with Sam. "Miss Liberty doesn't look too bad," he said. "Just blurred around the edges. And her crown is crooked."

As they watched, the back of Miss Liberty's head melted. Her crown fell onto the ice. A few moments later she dropped her book. It wasn't a real book, Oliver noticed. Just cardboard.

"Hey, Moffitt, give me a hand."

Oliver looked up. Rusty's cardboard fence was lying on the ice. He was trying to shove his car onto a piece of cardboard. "The ice is thinner out here," he said. "I've got to move the car."

Oliver ran over to help. He and Rusty gave the car a big shove. It slid onto the cardboard—and kept going, dragging the cardboard with it. Crack! The thin ice gave way under the weight. The car floated for a moment, held up by the cardboard. Then it slowly began to sink, until all that was left were two pie plates floating on the surface of the pond. Oliver couldn't take his eyes away from the watery grave.

"Moffitt! Watch out! The ice is cracking!" yelled Rusty.

Too late! *Crack!* The ice broke beneath Oliver's feet. The next thing Oliver knew, he was floundering around in icy water.

"Help!" he shouted. The cold felt like a vise. He couldn't breathe. He was beginning to sink. He pumped his arms and legs to stay afloat.

"I'll go get help," he heard Rusty shout.

Oliver's clothes soaked up the water. They were dragging him down. He could barely tread water now. His arms felt as if they were wrapped in lead.

"I'm drowning," he shouted. His head went under.

He shoved his legs against the water that was sucking him down. His head popped out. He flailed his arms. "Help!" he shouted again.

Then everything seemed to be happening in slow motion. He could see Sam. She was run-

ning, but it seemed to take her forever to reach Miss Liberty. She grabbed the hockey stick, whirled, and raced back. "Hold on," she shouted. "I'm coming."

Oliver sank below the water again. He was tired. Maybe he should just let himself sink. "Once more," he told himself. With great effort he pumped his sodden legs. Sam was kneeling on the ice. She was holding something out to him. He grabbed it tight. The hockey stick, he remembered. Sam pulled him closer to the edge of the broken ice. Oliver lifted one knee and pushed himself up and over. Sam grabbed his shoulders, and he clambered all the way out.

He lay there for a moment, then heard Pompom's barking from the shore. Oliver stood up. His legs were shaking.

"You must be freezing," Sam said. "You've got to get home and get warm fast."

Oliver shuddered in his dripping clothes. He and Sam ran to the shore. Sam picked up Pompom and put him into her basket. Oliver, teeth chattering, got on his bicycle. They pushed off together and raced for Oliver's house.

Once there, Oliver ran upstairs. He threw off his clothes and stood under a hot shower until he stopped shivering. Then he went into his room. He put on flannel-lined jeans, a T-shirt, and a sweatshirt. Back in the bathroom, he scooped up his soggy clothes and ran downstairs to join Sam and Pom-pom.

"Are you okay?" Sam asked.

Oliver dashed for the cellar. "Got to put these

in the dryer," he said. "Don't want Mom to know what happened." Sam nodded. Pom-pom ran after him.

"Wake up, stupid," Oliver heard as he headed down the cellar stairs.

"Igor! Where are you?" Oliver looked around. The clothes were dripping. He went over to the dryer. The door was already open. Oliver began to shove his clothes in. But the clothes started coming out. Something was inside!

Oliver bent down and peered in.

"Wake up, stupid," he heard.

Oliver threw the wet clothes on the floor just as Igor stuck his head out of the dryer. He tried to get out, but his claws kept slipping on the metal. Igor was stuck inside.

Oliver made his hand into a fist. Igor climbed on.

"Igor! Am I glad to see you," Oliver said.

"Bad boy," said Igor.

"You can say that again," Oliver said. "Stay there while I put these clothes in." Oliver set his arm on top of the dryer so Igor could stand on it. Then he picked up the wet clothes and stuffed them in the dryer. Igor flew off the dryer and toward the cellar steps. Oliver shut the dryer door and turned on the machine.

"Ah-liv-va!"

"I'm coming, Sam," Oliver yelled. He scooped Igor into his arms and ran up the stairs. "What's the matter?"

"Nothing! I didn't say anything," Sam said. "Hey look! It's Igor. You found him! Hooray!" She whirled and turned a couple of cartwheels.

Oliver laughed. "Well, if you didn't call my name, then who did?"

"Ah-liv-va!" said Igor.

"Igor! You said my name!" He turned to Sam. "Did you hear him?"

"That's terrific," said Sam. "But where did you find him?"

"In the dryer. When you took the shopping bag with the sheepskin coat the other day, he must have gotten in. You actually brought him here! Then somehow Igor found his way to the cellar. Now I remember. Pom-pom tried to get me to go down there. Anyway, the boiler keeps the room nice and warm. When Igor was squawking, the dryer was like an echo chamber. No wonder we could hear him all over the house."

"Ah-liv-va," said Igor. He jumped out of Oliver's arms. His eye was on Pom-pom.

Pom-pom ran under a chair. "Yap-yap."

"Bad boy," said Igor. He stalked over to the chair and peered under it. Pom-pom growled. "Stupid," said Igor.

Oliver spotted the shopping bag next to the sofa. Mrs. Moffitt had put the leftover pieces of sheepskin into the bag.

"Let's use the shopping bag to carry Igor *back* to the Kirkbys," Oliver said. He picked up the parrot and tucked him into the bag. "I've got to go over there later."

Holding Pom-pom tightly, Sam opened the front door. "It's gettting really warm. Let's go back to Great Pond first," she said.

"Okay," said Oliver. "It's on the way."

They ran down the porch steps. Sam put Pom-pom into her basket. Oliver put Igor in his and tucked the sheepskin around him. They raced for Great Pond.

Would Miss Liberty still be on her pedestal?

CHAPTER
9

As Sam and Oliver came close to Great Pond, they heard sirens. Then they saw an ambulance, a couple of fire engines—and a big crowd of people.

"What's going on?" said Sam, waving to Kim and Jennifer.

"Maybe they came to see the contest," Oliver suggested.

He and Sam parked their bicycles on the muddy grass.

"Oliver! Sam!" Josh and Matthew came running over. "There's been some kind of accident on the ice."

"Oh, no!" said Sam.

"What will they do about the sculpture contest?" Oliver asked.

"We don't know," Matthew said. "We can't get through the crowd."

"Well, I'm going to find out," Sam said. "Coming, Oliver?"

Oliver stepped away from his bike. "Stay," he told Pom-pom. Then he peeked inside the sheepskin coat, making sure Igor couldn't fly out of the basket. Igor was sitting tight. "Matthew, can you keep an eye on these guys?"

"Sure," Matthew and Josh both said.

Sam had already run out onto the ice. It was still solid near the shore. Policemen were trying to hold the crowd back from the hole in the ice where Rusty's car had sunk.

"What happened, officer?" Oliver heard someone call to a policeman.

"Some kid called the emergency number. Said his friend fell through the ice. Too late now. The boy must be drowned."

"How awful," Oliver said to Sam.

The policeman pointed to a van that came roaring up. "Look, here come the TV people."

The doors of the van swung open, and a camera crew dashed out. Leading them was a blond woman with a microphone in her hand.

"That's Kathy Kellogg," Sam said. "We watch her on the news every night."

"Where's the boy who saw it all?" Kathy Kellogg asked as her crew plunged through the crowd.

Oliver and Sam tagged along behind. They had a harder time pushing through the crowd. The cameras were set up and rolling by the time they reached the front row.

"Okay, Rusty," Oliver heard Kathy Kellogg say, "just tell us exactly what happened."

Oliver squirmed around a fat man's legs to see Rusty standing in front of the cameras beside the fire chief. His hat was in his hand. He looked as if he were trying hard not to cry.

"We were both in the contest, and we came out here to save our sculptures from melting," Rusty said. "He came out to help me. But then the ice started breaking . . . everything happened so fast. . . ."

Oliver turned to Sam. "You don't think—" he whispered.

"Shhhh," Sam whispered back.

"Was he a good friend?" Kathy Kellogg asked with a sympathetic smile.

"He wasn't as smart as I am, and we always had fights, but he was really all right." Rusty twisted his hat in his hands as he turned to look up at the sky. "Poor Oliver—"

The words caught in his throat when he saw Oliver staring at him. For a second Rusty looked like he'd just seen a ghost. Then he started to get angry. "You big jerk!" he yelled. "What do you think you're doing here?"

"Rusty, I don't understand. . . ." said Kathy Kellogg.

"He didn't drown at all, the big phony. He's standing right over there!"

When Oliver saw the cameraman turning toward him, he ducked into the crowd. His mother always watched the news after dinner. If she saw him on tonight's show, he would be in big trouble.

Oliver sighed. "No sooner do I get out of one mess," he thought, "than I fall into another."

The cameraman gave up on scanning for Oliver and focused on Kathy and Rusty. Oliver peeked through the crowd again.

Now the fire chief had a firm grip on Rusty's

shoulder. ". . . severe penalties for false alarms," he was saying.

"Wait a minute!" Sam stepped forward. "This is the way it happened." She told the story of how Oliver had fallen in, how Rusty ran to get help, and how she pulled Oliver out with the hockey stick. She pointed to Miss Liberty, and the cameraman turned to get a shot. Oliver pushed to the front again.

"So, we don't have a hero. We have a heroine." Now Kathy Kellogg was holding her microphone out to Sam, trying to get a *new* story.

"You *do* have a hero, Miss Kellogg! Rusty Jackson is a hero too," Sam said. "He ran for *help*. He did what he thought was right."

"I shouldn't have wasted my time." Rusty stared at Oliver. "Jerk," he said again. "He's not even wet!" The fire chief let Rusty go.

"We took him home to get him dried off," Sam went on.

"Great!" muttered Rusty. "If I had stayed, I could've been a hero. Instead, a dumb girl gets the credit. And they make *me* look dumb. On *television*." He stalked off, still grumbling.

Sam and Oliver looked at each other and shrugged.

"We'll have to cut out that last bit," Kathy Kellogg told her cameraman. "Nobody says 'dumb girl' on *my* show!"

"I think we may as well cut the whole story," said the cameraman. "Nothing happened. Nobody drowned!"

"Hey, look," Sam said. "The judges are here

for the snow-sculpture contest. Why don't you cover *that* story?"

A big black car had pulled up beside the kids and the bicycles. Across the ice, Oliver could hear a voice squawking, "Wake up, stupid!"

Two men in business suits got out of the car, along with Ms. Callahan, Oliver and Sam's teacher, and Mr. Thompson, the principal of the school.

"Why not?" said Kathy Kellogg. "At least we'll have *some* kind of a story." She and the cameraman raced over to the judges. Sam and Oliver followed.

"I did *not* call you stupid," Oliver heard Mr. Thompson say.

"Well, who did?" asked one of the judges. "I distinctly heard it."

"Oliver! Sam! How nice to see you," said Ms. Callahan. "We came to judge the snow sculptures. It's a shame about the thaw. That's why we're here a few hours early. We wanted to see all the sculptures before they melt."

Oliver smiled at Ms. Callahan. "They're over there," he said, pointing to what was left of Jennifer's worms, Josh's robot, Mr. Karate, and Miss Liberty.

"Nothing here but a bunch of snow mounds," said the first judge.

"That big grape-juice blot looks interesting," said Mr. Thompson. "I wonder what it was."

Kim and Jennifer came hurrying up. "Purple worms," Jennifer said with pride.

"Melted purple worms," said the other judge.

82

He walked up to Matthew's karate man. He was lying on his back, his head in a puddle of water.

"Karate man, huh?" the judge said after Matthew told him what the heap was. "Looks like he took a fall. Ha-ha-ha." He walked over to Josh's robot.

"And what is this?" asked Ms. Callahan.

"Can't you tell?" said Josh.

"It must be a robot," said Ms. Callahan. "Right?"

Josh gathered the pair of light bulbs that had fallen from the mound of snow surrounded by the blue scarf. He stuck them back in, looking at the first judge. The judge just shook his head and started walking toward Miss Liberty.

The statue's head had shrunk and was sitting on a big blurred pile of snow. Oliver squinted. Could it work?

He whispered something to Sam. She ran for the shore. Meanwhile Oliver bent down and picked up Miss Liberty's crown. He tore off one of the aluminum points and stuck it on the face.

Sam ran back, handing Oliver two flat stones.

He placed them on either side of the point and stepped back.

Mr. Thompson arrived. "This one must have been a good size," he said. "There's still a lot left." He turned to Oliver. "What is it?"

"The great snowy owl," Oliver said. "Right, Sam?"

She nodded. "Right," she said. "The great snowy owl."

"Well, it's the only sculpture that looks like

anything," said the second judge. He took another look at Josh's robot. Josh was wringing out the blue scarf. He picked up the light bulbs and put them into his pocket.

The judges went into a huddle.

A few moments later Ms. Callahan came back with a big smile. "Since your sculpture is the only one we can call a *sculpture*, the judges have decided to award you first prize. Congratulations."

Oliver reached for the envelope, but Sam got to it first. "Now you owe me only fifteen dollars," she whispered.

Kathy Kellogg and her cameraman came in for a close-up.

"Speech! Speech!" everyone shouted.

Sam smiled at the camera. "Thank you," she said. "We all worked very hard on our sculptures. I think we all deserve a prize. Rusty Jackson made a beautiful car, but it sank. . . ."

Oliver looked around. No Rusty.

"So," Sam went on. "I'm offering a prize. Let's all go to the Quick Shoppe for ice cream. My treat."

The judges and TV people all hurried off. "Which story do you think is better?" Oliver heard Kathy Kellogg ask. "The contest or the kid who fell in the water?"

"They both seem pretty dumb to me," said her cameraman. "My feet are wet."

Oliver stared at Miss Liberty. He shrugged. She *did* look like a great snowy owl.

"Are you coming?" asked Sam.

"Guess not," Oliver said. "I've got to take Igor back to the Kirkbys. Thanks anyway."

"That was quick thinking about the owl," Sam whispered. "We wouldn't have won the prize without you." She headed for the shore. Oliver followed.

Jennifer, Kim, Josh, and Matthew were waiting near their bicycles. Jennifer was sneezing.

"What's wrong with me?" Jennifer asked.

"Wake up, stupid!" a muffled voice came from the bag.

Jennifer jumped back with another sneeze.

"Can you do me a favor?" Oliver said to Sam. "I can't carry both Igor and Pom-pom in my basket. Would you take Pom-pom with you? Give him my share of the ice cream."

"It's a deal," said Sam. All the kids got on their bicycles and rode off.

"Wake up, Ah-liv-va," said Igor.

Oliver peeked in at the parrot and grinned. It wasn't such a bad day after all. He'd found Igor and taught him to say his name. And the great snowy owl idea meant he'd won his bet with Rusty.

"Bad boy," said Igor.

"Good bird," said Oliver as he hopped on his bicycle and headed for the Kirkby house. Maybe birds weren't so bad after all.

CHAPTER
10

Pom-pom lay asleep on the floor under Igor's cage. Every now and then he opened an eye as if to check that the parrot was safely locked up. It was Sunday, the last day of Oliver's vacation. And his last day as bird-sitter. The Kirkbys were due home any minute.

Oliver checked the aviary one more time. The new glass panel looked as if it had always been there. He'd hung up a new piece of cuttlebone. All the water bottles sparkled with fresh water. The seed and grit cups were full. He'd washed the plastic rug in the tub earlier. It was spotless.

Igor had his head under his wing. He'd just finished watching *Bye-Bye Birdland*, and like Pom-pom, was taking a nap. Everything was in perfect order.

Oliver was so nervous he couldn't sit still. He'd spent the morning cleaning and polishing his mother's antique birdcage. It looked beautiful sitting by the door, ready to be taken home.

Oliver heard a car pull into the driveway. He looked out the window. Mrs. Kirkby had gotten out of the car. She was carrying a cardboard box and what looked like a spear. Mr. Kirkby was unloading suitcases from the trunk.

Oliver opened the front door and ran down the steps.

"Welcome back," he shouted.

Mrs. Kirkby smiled. "How are my babies?" she asked.

"Everything okay with the flying circus?" said Mr. Kirkby. He slammed the trunk lid.

"No problem," said Oliver. He picked up a suitcase and followed the Kirkbys into the house.

"Hawaii was beautiful," Mrs. Kirkby said, "but there's no place like home." She set the spear against the wall near the aviary. Oliver studied it. The spear had a long metal point; the heavy, dark wood was carved with designs. One design looked like a kangaroo.

"Australian aborigine," said Mr. Kirkby. "I bought it in Hawaii." He set down his suitcases and picked up the spear.

"And look what I've got," Mrs. Kirkby said. She opened the cardboard box, reached in, and gently brought out a bird with a red and yellow face and a crest. "It's a cockatiel," she said, stroking its head.

She held it out to Oliver. When he hesitated, she took his hand and put his finger on the bird's head. Oliver gently stroked it.

"Isn't he wonderful?" asked Mrs. Kirkby. "His name is Hilo. Cockatiels are peace-loving birds. They get along very well with finches."

She took the bird and went over to the aviary. "This is your new home, Hilo," she said. She slid open the glass panel. "Go ahead, fly," she said to the bird. She tossed it into the air. It flew from her wrist onto a branch. Swaying, Hilo looked around at his new home.

Still holding the spear, Mr. Kirkby walked over. But as he moved, the shaft of the spear hit Oliver's birdcage. *BONNNNNNNG!* The brass cage rang like a giant gong.

Mr. Kirkby turned at the noise. His spear swept out and hit a lamp. And when he whirled to catch the lamp, the tip of the spear smashed right into the aviary.

Once again Oliver watched, frozen, as the glass shattered and fell.

"Not again!" he groaned.

"My babies!" Mrs. Kirkby screamed. "Hilo! Are you all right!"

Casper and Jasper strolled out of the aviary and under a chair. Pom-pom woke up and began to bark.

Oliver grabbed Pom-pom's collar. He turned to Mr. Kirkby, who was examining the point of the spear.

"Not damaged," he said. "That's a relief."

"I'll call the glazier," said Mrs. Kirkby. She walked into the kitchen.

"But the glass—" Oliver began.

"Oh, that." Mr. Kirkby seemed to notice the broken glass for the first time. "Don't worry about that! It's insured for breakage." He laughed. "And a good thing too. We must break it once a month—at least."

Oliver looked up. E and T were flying around the living room. Miss Tootsie, the canary, landed

on a lamp and began to sing. Hilo sat on his branch inside the aviary and looked worried. Pom-pom jumped down from Oliver's arms and ran to the door. He scratched on it to be let out. Whenever flying birds came by, he ducked. Finally, he crawled under the sofa.

Mrs. Kirkby came back into the living room. "Luke, the glazier's son, will be here in an hour," she said. "Thank goodness for his emergency service." She gazed at the birds flying around the room. "Oh, well, they needed the exercise," she said. "We'll catch them later."

She turned to Oliver. "It looks as if you've done a superb job. The birds look so healthy and well-fed," she said. "Frank, give Oliver his wages. He's earned them."

Mr. Kirkby set the spear down on the mantel. "It'll look great up there over the fireplace," he said. He dug out his wallet and handed Oliver several bills. "Thanks for a great job," he told Oliver.

"It wasn't anything—" Oliver began.

Mrs. Kirkby walked up to Igor's cage. "Did you miss me?" she asked.

"*Ah-liv-va!*" Igor squawked.

"Frank! Did you hear that?" Mrs. Kirkby said. "Igor said 'I love you.'" She turned to Oliver and gave him a hug. "You're a genius. You've finally taught him to say something nice." She motioned to Mr. Kirkby. "Give Oliver a bonus!"

"But—" Oliver began, and stopped. He took the money from Mr. Kirkby. Shouldn't he tell the Kirkbys that Igor was saying "Oliver," not "I love you"?

"Wake up, stupid," interrupted Igor.

Oliver grinned. He held out the money to Mr. Kirkby. "He's not saying 'I love you.' He's saying my name, 'Oliver.' "

Mr. Kirkby waved the money away. "Doesn't matter. If we hear 'I love you' and you hear 'Oliver,' it's still an improvement."

Oliver looked down at the money in his hand. He now had enough to pay back his mother and Sam—and the phone bill.

He looked up at the Kirkbys. Mrs. Kirkby was holding Hilo and stroking his head. Mr. Kirkby had his arm around his wife's shoulder.

"Guess we better sweep up the glass," Mr. Kirkby said. Mrs. Kirkby nodded.

Oliver put on his coat. Then he reached under the sofa and dragged out Pom-pom by his collar.

As he put on Pom-pom's turtleneck, he said to Mrs. Kirkby, "My mom said to thank you for the sheepskin jacket. But it's too warm to wear today. He really likes it though."

"I'm glad to hear that. You'll have to bring Pom-pom over again so I can see the coat on him. I'll bake cookies, and we can watch *Hula Birds on Parade*. I bought a new tape for Igor in Hawaii."

Oliver grinned. He snapped on Pom-pom's leash. "You bet," he said. "But school starts tomorrow."

"Come over after school then. How about Wednesday? And bring a friend if you like."

"Thanks, Mrs. Kirkby. This has been one of

the most interesting pet-care jobs I've had. I really learned a lot."

He picked up his mother's antique cage. Mrs. Kirkby ran her fingers across the top. "What a beautiful cage," she said. "Is that the one you got your mother for Christmas?"

Oliver nodded. "How did you know?"

"She told me." Mrs. Kirkby put her hand on the doorknob. "They don't make them like that anymore. Would you like a bird for it? We're expecting some little ones in the spring."

Oliver stared at E and T, who were flying around the room. Miss Tootsie was no longer sitting on the lamp. He could see two more birds on the curtain rod. He wondered if Miss Tootsie was in the fireplace.

He shook his head. "Thanks for the offer. But I think my mom would rather use the cage for a plant."

Mrs. Kirkby opened the door a crack, and Oliver and Pom-pom squeezed through. "Let me know if you change your mind," she said. She shut the door quickly.

A half hour later, when Oliver turned onto his street, he spotted a familiar bicycle in front of his house.

"Oh, no," he groaned. "Rusty!"

"Hey, Moffitt," Rusty said. "I've been looking for you. You know, I would've won the contest. But you shoved my 1956 Chevrolet into the water."

Oliver's mouth dropped open. He should have

expected Rusty to give him an argument about the contest.

"The thaw—" Oliver began.

"Just kidding," Rusty said. He dug into his pocket. "Ten bucks, just like I promised. I'm glad you didn't drown."

Oliver's mouth dropped open again. It was the first time he could ever remember Rusty saying something nice! "For a second there I thought you were calling off the bet." It was all Oliver could think of to say.

Rusty shrugged. "The other night, when my mom saw the news, she heard Sam talking about how you fell into the pond. Mom said that the kid who ran for help did the right thing. Then she heard Sam mention my name. She gave me a big hug, and said I was a hero."

"Well, you were. Sort of," said Oliver. "When my mom saw the news, she made me take another hot shower."

"Serves you right," Rusty said, grinning. He hopped on his bicycle. "I still say you and Sam had a dumb idea. It never would have worked."

"Oh, yeah?" said Oliver.

"Yeah," said Rusty.

"Wanna bet?" asked Oliver.

Pom-pom began to bark. "Um, never mind," Oliver said quickly. His calculator was safe. He looked at the ten-dollar bill and turned it over to make sure it was real.

"You won this time, Moffitt," Rusty said. "But someday . . ."

Oliver looked at the birdcage in his other hand. Maybe he could lock up his valuables in it. No, he decided. Ten dollars would buy his mother a very nice plant.

Rusty stopped and turned to face Oliver. "You know something? I always used to think you were for the birds. But after this, well . . ."

"What?" Oliver asked.

"Now I *know* it." Rusty cracked up at his own joke. "See you in school tomorrow."

"Right," said Oliver.

He went inside with a contented sigh. Vacation was finally over. Now he could get some rest.